Iktomi
and the
Coyote

I'm looking good.
I AM good-looking.

Hi kids! I'M IKTOMI!
That white guy, Paul Goble, is telling my stories again.
Only Native Americans can tell Native American stories.
So, let's not have anything to do with them. Huh?
You're cool kids! You're GREAT!!

Iktomi's other misadventures:
Iktomi and the Berries
Iktomi and the Boulder
Iktomi and the Buffalo Skull
Iktomi and the Buzzard
Iktomi and the Ducks

and the books not about Iktomi:
Crow Chief
Remaking the Earth

also:
Adopted by the Eagles
Beyond the Ridge
Buffalo Woman
Custer's Last Battle
Death of the Iron Horse
Dream Wolf
The Fetterman Fight
The Friendly Wolf
The Gift of the Sacred Dog
The Girl Who Loved Wild Horses
The Great Race
Hau Kola—Hello Friend
(an autobiography for children)
Her Seven Brothers
I Sing for the Animals
The Legend of the White Buffalo Woman
Lone Bull's Horse Raid
The Lost Children
Love Flute
The Return of the Buffaloes
Star Boy

Iktomi
and the
Coyote

a Plains Indian story

told and illustrated
by PAUL GOBLE

Orchard Books   New York

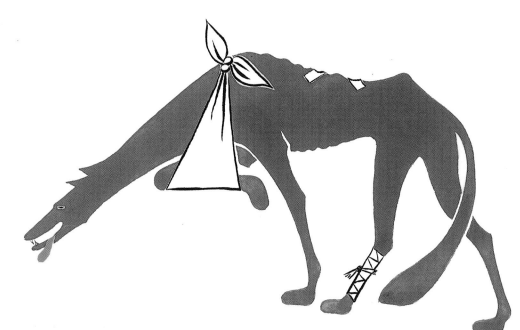

GON 2 THE SKOOL

for Ben Goble

References

Maurice Boyd, *Kiowa Voices—Myths, Legends and Folktales*, Vol. II, Texas Christian University Press, Fort Worth, 1983 (185, 190); J. Frank Dobie, *The Voice of the Coyote*, Hammond, Hammond & Co Ltd, London, 1950 (277); George Bird Grinnell, *Blackfoot Lodge Tales*, Charles Scribner's Sons, New York, 1892 (155–58, 171); Gerald Hausman, ed., *Prayer to the Great Mystery— The Uncollected Writings and Photography of Edward S. Curtis*, St. Martin's Press, New York, 1995 (109); A. L. Kroeber, *Cheyenne Tales*, *The Journal of American Folk-Lore*, Vol. XIII, New York, 1900 (168); Walter McClintock, *The Old North Trail—Life, Legends and Religion of the Blackfeet Indians*, Macmillan, London, 1910 (338); Darnell Davis Rides at the Door, *Napi Stories*, Blackfeet Heritage Program, Browning, 1979 (33); Stith Thompson, *Tales of the North American Indians*, Indiana University Press, Bloomington, 1929 (162, 298); Clark Wisler and D. C. Duvall, *Mythology of the Blackfoot Indians*, Anthropological Papers of the American Museum of Natural History, Vol. II, New York, 1908 (25–27); Zitkala-Sa, *Old Indian Legends*, Ginn, Boston, 1901 (27).

Copyright © 1998 by Paul Goble. All rights reserved. No part of this book may be reproduced or transmitted in any form or by any means, electronic or mechanical, including photocopying, recording, or by any information storage or retrieval system, without permission in writing from the Publisher. Orchard Books, 95 Madison Avenue, New York, NY 10016. Manufactured in the United States of America. Printed by Barton Press, Inc. Bound by Horowitz/Rae. The text of this book is set in 22 point ITC Zapf Book Light. Library of Congress Cataloging-in-Publication Data. Goble, Paul. Iktomi and the coyote : a Plains Indian story / told and retold by Paul Goble.   p. cm. Includes bibliographical references. Summary: After tricking some prairie dogs into becoming his dinner, Iktomi is himself outwitted by Coyote. Asides and questions printed in italics may be addressed by the storyteller to listeners, encouraging them to make their own remarks about the action. ISBN 0-531-30108-7 (trade : alk. paper).—ISBN 0-531-33108-3 (lib. bdg. : alk. paper) 1. Indians of North America—Great Plains—Folklore. 2. Iktomi (Legendary character)—Juvenile literature. 3. Tales—Great Plains. [1. Iktomi (Legendary character)—Legends. 2. Indians of North America—Great Plains—Folklore. 3. Folklore—Great Plains.] I. Title. E78.G73G629 1998 398.2'089'97—dc21 98-11082

The illustrations are India ink and watercolor on Oram & Robinson [England] Limited Watercolor Board, reproduced in combined line and halftone. 10 9 8 7 6 5 4 3 2 1   Book design by Paul Goble

About Iktomi

The Trickster's name in Lakota is *Iktomi,* meaning spider. He is a man with spiderlike traits, clever but untrustworthy. In this story, he meets Coyote, equally clever and untrustworthy. The Trickster appears with different names and the story details change with the times and to suit different regions, but the themes, the ideas, are shared by Native American storytellers all over the continent. Trickster stories are among the oldest North American stories, uniquely rooted in this land.

In Buffalo Days, Iktomi was a mirror of human nature with its range of infinite possibilities, from the divine to degradation. Nowadays he has been relegated mostly to his Trickster role, his other aspects having been forgotten amid modern world pressures. People often talk about "Iktomi Power" when they talk about abuses of gambling, alcohol, and drugs, but Iktomi Power can also be power for good. There are stories that recall how Iktomi, the Creator's helper, shaped the buttes, lakes, and rivers, and how when people were new on Earth he taught them useful things, like making fire and bows and arrows.

Nearly forty years ago, as I was sitting with Edgar Red Cloud, Lakota, in the shade of cottonwood trees at the powwow ground in Pine Ridge, South Dakota, Edgar picked up a leaf and drew my attention to its shape. It had given Iktomi the idea for tipis, he said, and by folding the leaf Iktomi invented moccasins. Once I showed Edgar a stone arrowhead I had bought at the trading post and asked if anyone still made them. People did not make those, he answered; Iktomi made them. Edgar knew it was manmade, but its beauty and usefulness, like tipis and moccasins, could only have been conceived by Iktomi. "He is rather a superman," Edgar said. "Our people look to him. He has a life and ways that we still tell about today." Then, with a twinkle in his eye, he recounted one of the funny stories about Iktomi the Trickster!

A Note for the Reader

You may know the Trickster by another name: Old Man Coyote, Napi, Wihio, Glooscap, Nanabozo, etc. Instead of "Iktomi," use the name you know.

Stories about the Trickster have always been told with "audience participation." When the text changes to gray italic, readers and listeners may want to make their own comments. Iktomi's thoughts, printed in small type, might break the flow of the story and can be read when looking at the pictures.

Iktomi was walking along. . . .

*Do you remember that every story
about Iktomi starts like this?*

I won't take the car today.
I look like a real chief.
I AM a real chief!

My warbonnet and trailer
(Eagle-friendly feathers
made of dyed domestic
goose)

My otter fur
(imitation)
necklace
with mirrors

Iktomi
and the
Ducks
PAUL GOBLE

My book
about me

Iktomi
and the
Buzzard
PAUL GOBLE

My blanket

My trade-cloth leggings

My moccasins

Iktomi was walking along.

"Hi! I'm Iktomi. You know me.
Yesterday I was at the White House.
The President needed my advice."

? ? ?

"That was yesterday. Today I'm going
to the school to read to the kids.
I'll read them these books, which tell all
about my brave deeds and generosity.
Everyone has read them. I'm famous."

*We know Iktomi is famous —
but it's not for brave deeds or
generosity, is it?
Do you think he can read?*

"I'm wearing my traditional clothes.
Today I feel just g-r-e-a-t. I look good.
The kids will be impressed.
I know I look good, because I am
dressed like I am in these books."

*Iktomi always thinks such a lot of
himself, doesn't he?*

"The kids will see how the ancestors
dressed, l-o-n-g, long ago . . .
although it has to be said:
I do look better than they did."

Yes?

Another book
about me

How did my ancestors
tell stories if they had no books?

"I'll tell the kids how we lived in Buffalo Days. I'm the only elder left."
Do you think he lived in those days, more than a hundred years ago?

Is there a powwow
somewhere?
I want to dance.

I'm an elder,
so I must be wise.

Am I hearing voices?
They put you in the
hospital for that.

"What's that?"
Iktomi heard laughter . . .
and high-pitched singing. . . .

He looked this way—and that way.
He could *not* see anyone.
Then he heard it again!
"Oh! Look! It's the prairie dogs!
Hmmmm. . . .
I'm real hungry for prairie dog!"
*They say the only time Iktomi does not
think about food is when he is eating!*
"There's *nothing* more tasty than baked
prairie dog!" he said to himself.
Really?
"Now . . . how shall I catch them?"

I should tell you, dear readers,
Iktomi made a mistake:
he gave them the name "prairie dogs."
But they aren't dogs at all. . . .
They are really ground squirrels!

He crept stealthily toward them.
He thinks they haven't seen him!
They were playing a game, taking turns
being buried up to their necks
in the hot ashes of
their cooking fire.

I'm a great hunter—
it's in my ancestral blood.
I wish I had brought my AK-47.

They were singing a special song, which stopped them from getting burned. But when they could not stand the heat any longer, they called, and their friends quickly pulled them out.

They were laughing and having so much fun. Iktomi said,
"Oh my little brothers, what a great game: to be buried in the ashes and not get burned. I want to do it! Please bury me too."
"*Oh no,* Ikto!" they all answered.
"You would *burn!* First you have to learn our song so you won't be burned. Listen carefully to us!
After that we'll bury you in the ashes."
Aren't prairie dogs kind?

"All right," Iktomi said. "But I have an even better idea: let me cover *all* of you with ashes, *all at the same time!* That way your song will be so loud I'll be sure to hear it.
When you want me to pull you out, just *shout* for *out!*"
"Ikto has such *great* ideas!" they said.

. . . shout for *out. . . .*
I like rhyme.
I'm a poet.

I love Ikto.

Isn't Ikto nice!

He's so handsome.

A real gentleman.

He's lovely.

All the little prairie dogs quickly lay
down together, side by side like beans
in a pod.
Iktomi worked hard covering them up
with hot ashes, and all the while the
prairie dogs sang at the very tops of
their high-pitched voices.

Do you think Iktomi has
some mischief in mind?

"Just *shout* for *out!*" Iktomi chuckled
to himself, as he shoveled on more
ashes.

Ikto, you are really clever.
They've fallen for my idea—
all in a row!

Well ...
one less won't matter.

In a little while, the prairie dogs began crying to be pulled out, but Iktomi just worked all the harder, heaping on more and ever more ashes.

The prairie dogs implored him to take them out. One pleaded most piteously for her babies that were soon to be born.

You spotted her, didn't you?

"All right," Iktomi said, and he pulled her out. "Go and live. Then there'll always be more prairie dogs."

After that, Iktomi just hardened his heart and closed his ears to their screams . . . and the prairie dogs baked . . . to death. . . . Yaaaa . . .

*Isn't he **horrible?***

I HATE Iktomi!!

Since then, prairie dogs' tails have had burned-black tips. They will never again trust two-leggeds, or let them get close.

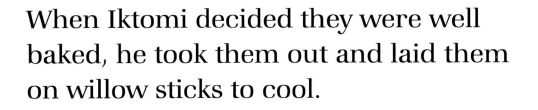

When Iktomi decided they were well
baked, he took them out and laid them
on willow sticks to cool.

*(If you should ever happen to burn
green willow sticks, you will notice
they are still soaked with grease.)*

He sat down on a rock.
His mouth was watering, and just as
he was going to take his first bite,
he caught sight of Coyote approaching.
"I try, but I can *never* like Coyote,"
he muttered to himself.

M-m-m-m. This is *gen-u-ine*
fast food!

Coyote's not my brother.
I don't have to
share *NOTHING*
with him.

Now Coyote looked very sad indeed, sick and starved, and he limped slowly and painfully on three legs.

You saw him on the previous page, didn't you? We like Coyote, don't we?

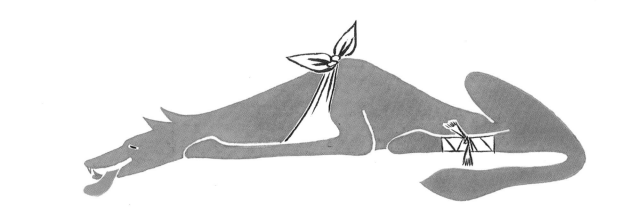

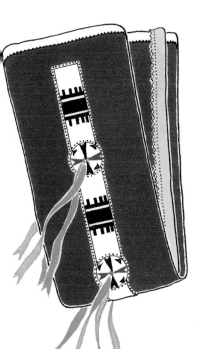

"Oh Ikto, my older brother, I'm feeling so weak, so weak," Coyote gasped. "Please give me some of your meat. I've had nothing to eat for so long, so long."
"Certainly *not!*" Iktomi answered hard-heartedly. "Not even one single bite. It's mine. *All of it. Go away!*"

But then Iktomi changed his mind.
"Well, yes, all right, I'm a fair man."
Hmmmmmm . . . ?
"I'll give you a chance. We'll gamble.
We'll race around that hill over there.
Winner eats all this meat."

Is that a fair race?
People shouldn't gamble, should they?

"Ah, yes, my younger brother,"
Iktomi added, "I can see you are not
quite in the very best of health.
To make it a *fair* race, I'll carry this
rock that I'm sitting on."
He put the rock in his blanket and
slung it over his shoulder.

I'd like to bet on this race!
If only my ancestors had had casinos. . . .

Fancy that silly Coyote thinking he could beat me!

Suddenly Iktomi called out:
"1!   2!   3!   GO!!"

He was off, running as fast as he could,
with the heavy rock swinging up and
down and hitting him in the back at
every step he took.
"Ikto! Wait! W-a-i-t," Coyote called
after him. But Iktomi took no notice.
"Ikto! Friend! Don't leave me."

When Iktomi started to run around the
other side of the hill, Coyote was far,
far behind.
"W-a-i-t f-o-r m-e!" he wailed
most piteously.

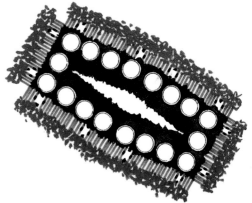

When Iktomi was out of sight behind
the hill, Coyote threw off all pretense.
He pulled off his bandages and rushed
back to eat up the prairie dogs.
He had only been pretending to be sick!

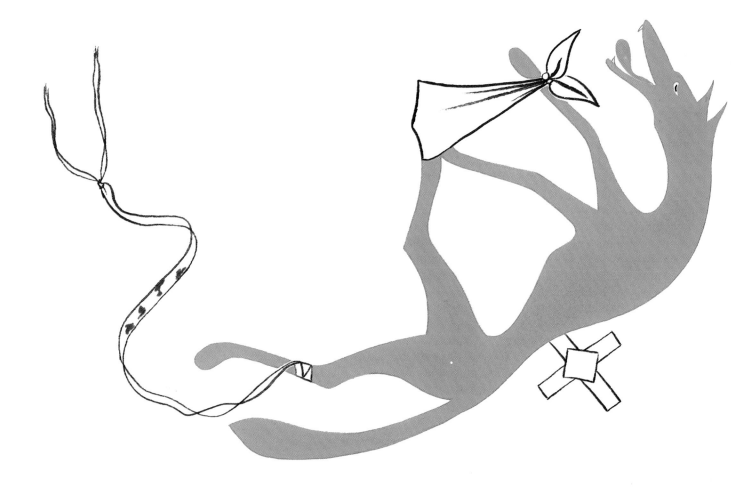

Crow

Eagle

In between mouthfuls, Coyote cried out for all his relations to hear:
"FOOD! Come and get it!"
His coyote relatives, everywhere, heard him and came running. His other relatives, Buzzard and Eagle, Crow and Magpie, joined in the feast too. Mouse cleaned up the pieces they dropped.

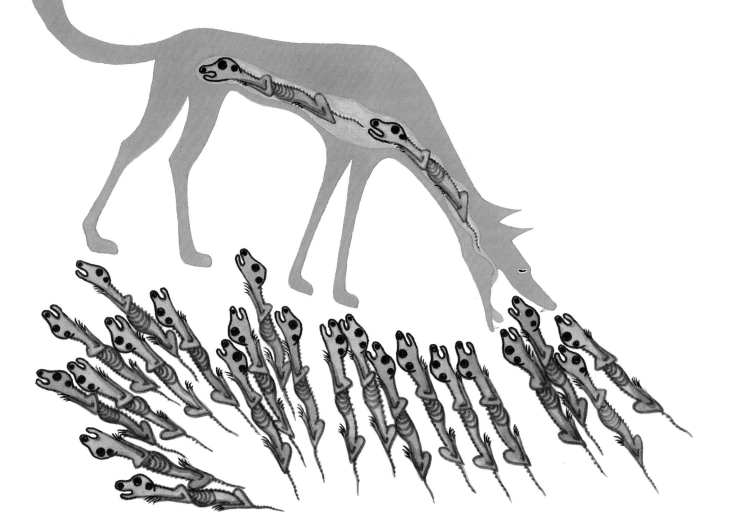

They must have all come
to cheer me winning.

When Iktomi appeared around the other
side of the hill, he saw he had been
tricked.

"Leave me some meat!" he called.

"Leave me some meat!"

Buzzard

Coyote relations

Magpie

Mouse

"That's—
not—
fair,"
Iktomi panted.
"You—
didn't—
leave me—
any.
You—
didn't—
give me—
a chance."

B . . . . . . s!
Anyway . . .
I never did like
prairie dog meat.

"I gave you as fair a chance as you gave the prairie dogs," said Coyote, grinning and licking his chops.
He staggered off, feeling he had eaten much too much.
"Just you wait," Iktomi warned him, "you thieving, mangy good-for-nothing. I'll get even with you!
Oh, but I *will!*"
Do you think so?

Burp-p-p-p-p-p

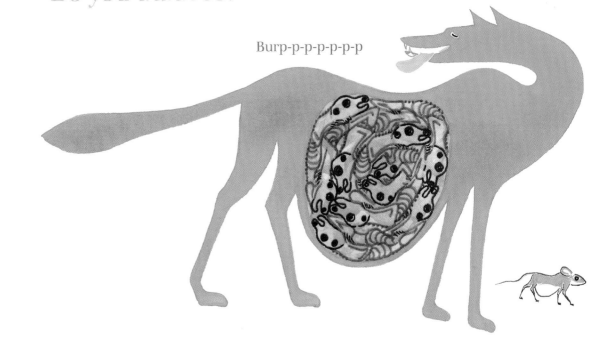

Let me THINK. . . .
WHAT was I going to do?
Yes! Of course!!
I'm HUNGRY!!!
I want
a double cheeseburger,
jumbo fries,
humongous pop.

Iktomi went on his way again. . . .

*Has anyone got an idea what he will
get up to next?*